american trash

14 SONGS AND A BOOK

A Daz Unlimited Production

In memory of
Richard "Dubie" Dubelman

Published by Daz Unlimited
Daz Unlimited
1093 Broxton Avenue
P.O. Box 523
Los Angeles, CA 90024

PUBLISHER'S NOTE
This is a work of fiction. Names, characters, places, and incidents
either are the product of the author's imagination or, are used ficti-
tiously, and any resemblance to actual persons, living or dead,
events, or locales is entirely coincidental.

SESAC/ASCAP

Contents

Chapter One

She wore a blue and white sundress that I bought her at the Salvation Army. I didn't pick it out. I just paid for it because she said it was comfortable, and I figured for three bucks, if you wear it twice it's worth it.

"Billy, if we had a child what would we call her?" she said in her strawberry voice. Normally, her voice was deep and rough from Marlboro Lights. But now her voice was like a blond-haired four-year-old boy. He wears overalls and eats wild strawberries on an upstate New York farm. He just picks one and eats it. He picks another and eats it. Picks another. It isn't good. Picks another.

"I don't know," I said, trying to prolong the moment.

"How about Magnolia?"

"Yeah, I like that."

But wait. Way before I started seeing her I got this Radio Shack his and hers alarm clock. It has two alarms, which I like because I can get up and turn off the alarm clock, go back to sleep, and wake up fresh ten minutes later. Ten minutes doesn't seem that long, but that's when I dream. Or, at least, that's when I have the dreams that I remember. The clock is digital; at night, it looks like two eyes staring at you. Her brown eyes highlight her face because she has orange hair. Her hair is like Mexican food: You start to really love it, but then you lose your sensitivity to less spicy stuff. My clock read 10:21 p.m. Where was she? She told me she'd call at 10:30. I stared at the white phone with the orange cord. My cord broke and the AT&T store was out of white, so I chose orange. I couldn't wait two weeks for a cord, and I didn't want to go to another phone store. Besides, who's going to kill me for having an orange cord?

Once, it was different. It was the smell. All the bad stuff was mosquito bites. I kissed her shoulder, I can't remember why. But the smell...when she came home from work she always smelled of fried food, like crisp well-done French fries made with three-day-old oil and grilled cheese sandwiches with extra American cheese and tons of butter to protect the bread from burning. When you pick up the tanned sandwich, your hands are covered with grease, but you just lick your fingers clean.

Her skin was like that. Like grape chapstick. It smells so good you want to eat it, but when you do, it tastes like chapstick.

"Hi," she said. Her voice was sexy in a childlike way. I rolled down the window.

"Hi," I answered, pretending I was Elvis Presley.

"Do you still love me?"

"I love you so much."

"Did you miss me, Billy?"

"Tons." I got out, kissed her upper lip gently, and opened the door for her. "You know, your voice sounds like a combination of Shirley Temple and Marilyn Monroe."

She laughed. I spun the tires. "You know your car sounds like Burt Reynolds."

"Yeah, but my car doesn't have hair transplants." Her smile rose to a crescendo and then into a laugh, and so I admit it, I laughed at my own joke.

"What do you wanna do?" I asked. She took a deep breath as if the doctor had said, "Take a deep breath, Rosanna. Good Girl."

"Well." She took off her shoes and stiffened her back. "I have to call my sister."

"Don't you want to get something to eat?"

"I'm not hungry, but I'll go with you."

"Forget it." I made a mental note to cancel the reservation at Le Rendezvous. "I have popcorn at the apartment, anyway."

"Okay, Jellybean."

We parked the car. While walking to the elevator, she put her hand behind her back. Then she flapped her hand opened and closed. I took her hand.

"I love you, Billy."

"You do?"

"Yes."

"How much?"

"A lot."

"Yea!" It was as though the Mets had come through in the bottom of the ninth—not the World Series, but an important game.

My apartment had her pink Samsonite make-up box on the floor. Yellow Adidas sweat pants hung across the bookcase and her black fishnet stockings were folded neatly on my bedside lamp. I had replaced one of two light bulbs in it with a green bulb. There were white Beverly Hills Hotel towels on the floor. I use a new towel every morning, but only because I have so many. Now you know it: I'm a towel thief. My faded blue jean jacket, my white robe that we shared, and her red socks lay on the brown leather couch. There was a Buddy Guy record on. I always need sound from the second I walk in to the second I leave; it sets the mood, I think. Understandably, she hates it.

I picked up the robe to hang it up in the bathroom. I remembered a shower we had taken together. She washed my back with Dial. She started to wash her neck.

"Let me." I took the soap and washed her neck, her upper chest, then her breasts.

"Underneath is most important," she said. "That's where they sweat."

Chapter Two

The light had just turned red. I really didn't feel like waiting. First of all, there was a Jerry Lee Lewis song on the radio. If you're driving around for the thrill of it and a good song comes on the radio, you just don't stop for red lights. Second, if you're driving around to let out aggression and a good song comes on the radio, you just *don't* stop for red lights. Third, I wanted to drive...

"Have you been drinkin', son?" said Officer Friendly as he flashed a light into my car. Not only was the light blinding, but it was also an invasion into my Cutlass.

"No, sir," I answered, but what I was thinking was, "No, sir, I haven't had anything to drink, but only because I have ulcers." (It's never been confirmed, but I'm sure because I can feel them.) "If, however, I could be drunk, I would be. But as it is, I can't get drunk, so no, sir, I have not been a-drinkin'."

"Step out of the car, son."

He thinks he's John Wayne.

"Son, I'm going to have to give you a ticket for going through a red light."

"Oh, shit. Can't you give me a break, Officer? I had a fight with my girlfriend."

"You shouldn'ta been drivin' if you weren't *emotionally stable*."

"Oh, Jesus," I said. "I can assure you I was perfect until I went to her apartment and found her sleeping with another man. What would you have done? Walked home?" Don't believe this. I'll admit it's sleazy, but I really didn't want a ticket.

"Hum," he said as he carefully pondered my story. I could sense Officer Friendly softening. I had to appeal to his emotions.

"And Officer, I'm a driver for the Volunteer Ambulance Corps. You can check it, if you want." I took a chance. Besides, who would he check with, and if he did find out what would he do, give me a ticket?

"God, I just can't get a ticket now! I'll lose my license, and if I lose my license, I'll lose my job delivering for Dan's Drugs. Can't you give me a break?" Once you sense your opponent's weakness, you have to put him away.

"Okay, son," he said. It's over—break out the champagne. "But the next time you get into a fight with your girlfriend and you feel less than *emotionally even-tempered*, you call yourself a cab." With this he grabbed his balls.

"Yes, sir."

"And don't run into me again, son."

Chapter Three

i

From when I was about ten, I used to hang out with Robby, Joe, and Richie.

Robby, you went to his house and you were alone. Joe, you went to his house and he got yelled at by his mother.

Richie, you went to his house and he laughed at his parents.

Robby Yarns was a strong but short boy, not really stocky because he actually had a good build. He had dirty blonde hair and blue eyes and forearms that looked like baseball bats. He was pretty wild, and his parents were pretty liberal—they gave him the keys to the house when he was ten because they didn't want to wait up for him.

Robby had a smell, not a bad one, but it wouldn't be unusual to see him wear a new Pittsburgh Steelers shirt for six days in a row, and then not see it until the next time he wore it for six days. And not only with the Steelers shirt, but with others, too; not all others, but definitely others.

Joe was much taller and bigger and even slightly mean at times, you know, the way kids are mean. For instance, when there was a display of artwork, Joe would destroy all the art that he thought was better than his. Then he would destroy his own, in order to avoid being suspected. I had to destroy mine, too, but mine was always terrible anyway.

He used to challenge Robby to races and athletic events, but he was always the bad guy. The sad thing is that he always wanted to be Robby, I think. Maybe we all did, except Robby.

Richie is the one I wanted to tell you about, because I never understood him myself. He was like me: a pretty good athlete, not great like Robby and Joe, but not bad at all really. He was cool. When you went to his house, his mother would yell at him, "Richie, where the devil are you?"

He would answer, "Where the devil?" sarcastically, and laugh.

One night his parents weren't home, so we went over there to watch *The Love Boat*. We never laughed at it, though. Not even when we were kids.

Joe would say, "Can I have some milk, Richie?"

And Rich would say, "Sure," with a smile, and get it. He would get it with a smile because he knew that the coolest thing he could do was get everybody everything they wanted and let you know with his smile that it was somewhat of a hassle, but that he would "gladly" do it for you. Also he would get it himself to try to be extra careful, so as not to really mess up his house.

And nobody ever hated Richie: not his parents, his friends, or even strangers.

ii

My father used to play this game with me. He's an executive at a Madison Avenue advertising agency. Part of his job is to make bids. The trick with bids is to justify as high a bid as you can, because you make commissions on them. My father always liked the idea of giving boldly high bids. Sometimes he would tell me about them, and I would always suggest he go higher. He would either agree, "I could do that. Yeah, I think so," or he would justify a lower bid. He'd giggle, "There are so many other bidders, they'll take the Young and Rubicam bid. I couldn't ask for that."

"But you're better than Young and Rubicam," I would

remind him.

"I don't know; they're just as good, really. I'm not so sure there's any big difference. What the hell, their ad might even be better."

I would retreat: "Yeah, I'm really not sure about all that."

Either way he answered, I gave him what he wanted. It was kind of fun, actually.

iii

With Rosanna, I didn't know what she wanted. And worse, I didn't know what I wanted.

Chapter Four

I know that I have neglected to mention some important details because I wanted you to know me. I had a nightmare. In the nightmare there was a beautiful painting of a sunset that I loved to get stoned to. I mean I was watching this sunset, and it was purple and orange and the saxophone was playing the blues. Not the sleazy blues of Chicago, but more like Phil Woods with his light green jazz tone like Tiffany eggs and cinnamon toast, and an old gentleman in a maroon smoking jacket. But the painter kept adding pinks and greens and blues that were beautiful, and I could smell fresh strawberries, and then the colors began to combine, and they kept getting darker until it turned to night. But not the warm cuddles of lovenight. More like the thick black paint of too many colors. Too much—the chintzy way out. And what would you do if your grandfather, you of his flesh and blood, took your baby daughter and masturbated her? You might pretend it didn't happen. If you thought, out of pure stupidity, that children don't remember and that, yes, most of her childhood was pleasant enough and papa was old and senile and he didn't know what he was doing anyfuckingway. I don't want to talk to you now. I want a drink.

She left her perfume bottle and an earring here.

iii

I noticed I'm eating less these days.

iv

I hadn't eaten deli for a couple of weeks. Sometimes I just forget about certain places for a while. Preoccupied. Don't get me wrong; this doesn't mean that I don't treasure them. I mean Sol 'n' Sol means a lot to me. I know it sounds silly to have an emotional attachment to a restaurant, but...

I get too committed to things. When I was six they wanted to take *H.R. Puff n' Stuff* off the air, and I made a sign and picketed. I had nowhere to picket except in front of the TV. My mom was a little puzzled, but she let me do it. Nothing happened, except a million years later I read in the paper that *H.R.* was suing Burger King for copyright infringement.

Anyway, I decided to get a corned beef sandwich. I was reading the *Enquirer* just to sort of drown my sorrows. It said something about a black bear who saved a human child from a forest fire.

"How you doing? I haven't seen you for a while." Sam is one of those people who always tries to be friendly, and sometimes you're not in the mood. He has a shake that's getting worse, and that makes me feel bad for him. Lately, I noticed he keeps getting more philosophical—telling me to go back to school.

"I've been working hard." But the truth is I hadn't been working much at all. I wished I had. At least it made me feel a little better to pretend that I had. Besides, I have to act responsibly.

"I have some nice brisket."

"No, I'll have a corned beef sandwich on a roll with cole slaw and mustard, and a grilled chopped liver on rye for her."

"For who?"

"What?"

"For who?"

I'd lost it. I didn't want to discuss my relationship with him. I could tell him someone would be here to meet me but when no one showed, it would look like I'd been stood up. I'll tell him I want to take it to go. That's what I meant.

"Someone may meet me here."

"Are you gonna wait, or just bring you yours first?"

"Bring them both, and if she's late I'll take it to go." I was a little tight on cash, but I didn't mind paying for it. To tell you the truth, I just wanted to look at it. Chopped liver is a strange food...something about Prometheus.

"And what are you gonna have to drink?"

v

If you read *Macbeth* you don't just say, "I read that play." You think about the rest of your life even if you don't want to.

vi

Close your eyes. Relax the muscles in your back. Take the tension out of your chest.

vii

Shakespeare and Rosanna get married and live in the East Village off love forever. I'll visit them in the spring and rape their children.

viii

When I was in eighth grade I had to read *Julius Caesar* for English. I was thinking about baseball and breasts at that point in my life, but a young energetic English teacher distracted me with Shakespeare. He acted it out so hard that he would sweat, and by the end of class he smelled like wet dog. His acting was big and corny the way a Big Mac seems when you compare it to a regular hamburger, but it captivated us. He also played us a British record of it featuring Paul Scofield. It broke up the monotony, but it didn't hold our attention like that Bugs Bunny English teacher. I started to think about Brutus and Caesar and Marc Anthony, and I bought into the idea that Brutus was a nice guy who was disgusted with Caesar. Marc Anthony was bad. As I started to get older I realized what Caesar had to face. *Et tu Brute*. Deserted by his closest friend. And it was brutal. So I understood where Brutus was disillusioned, but he also murdered his best friend—in fact almost a father figure. I haven't read or seen the play for years, but I think about it all the time. It's become one of those things that I just can't get my mind off of. And still it annoys me that I think about Rosanna all the time. Why? I think about Brutus all the time. He was rash. He should have talked to Caesar. But would Caesar have listened? And it would have cost the other conspirators their lives. But the word conspirators—and Brutus was a member. I almost wish I hadn't read the play. I mean where the hell am I for thinking about it all the time? Has it stopped me from being an asshole even once? Maybe I should think about work a little more often.

ix

My dog, Clemente, had the strangest routine. He would circle a spot before he would lie down. Perspective? No, just routine.

Chapter Five

"**M**y father has a car just like that." She was off. Excited and inspired, and even when I don't care what people are saying, I love to hear enthusiasm. I read an article in *Sports Illustrated* about those win-one-for-the-gipper speeches. Apparently, they don't work. You can't make a guy a better football player just by asking. In fact, sometimes a guy will get really up after one of those talks and end up hurting himself because he really wants to win. That's what the article said, but I don't believe that crap. So I didn't really follow what she said, but she was compelled, so I forced out a white smile.

"Nobody should be poor," she stressed. I agreed, raised my eyebrows, and nodded.

"Rosanna. I want to tell you something important, but..." I smiled. "I love you."

"I love you too, Billy. So much. I told you about my great uncle."

"The math guy from Cleveland?"

"No, my Great Uncle Alex owned a grocery store in Russia."

"Oh."

"Yeah, he was the dark brother. One day he found a rat in a barrel of olive oil. So he fished it out and sold the oil."

"That's terrible. He must have really needed money."

"Then his customers found out. It wasn't good publicity."

"His family was probably starving, and he had no way to make up for a whole barrel of oil. His family—maybe two little girls—that's what he was thinking of."

"Maybe."

ii

I began to avoid going out with friends, preferring, instead, to be with Rosanna alone. I used to go out often and drink vodka and go whoring. That sounds interesting; it isn't true, but I did like to be with her a lot.

iii

"Don't do this to yourself!" I said to myself. You see I had bought myself a used Betamax from an old friend—Bobby—who was leaving New Jersey. He had accepted the position of vice-president in charge of marketing at P&G in Cincinnati. I bought it off him for two hundred bucks and recorded all the old *Twilight Zones*. When I was alone I would watch the *Twilight Zone* for hours. Maybe two. Maybe four. Sometimes six. Usually an even number. That way, if I couldn't stop watching it, I'd have a set time to end at. Beginnings and endings, that's what I like. My day hasn't begun, for example, if I don't take a shower in the morning.

Chapter Six

i

Airline Representative
Smoking or non-smoking?

Rosanna   Billy
Smoking.   Non-smoking.

Airline Representative
Shall I seat you together?

Rosanna
I'm sitting in the smoking section.

Billy
Come on. Sit with me in the nice clean non-smoking section where you can still enjoy the fresh air and—

Rosanna
a man is still a man—

Airline Representative
While you two are deciding, I'm going to seat these people.

Billy
I've made my decision. Non-smoking.

Rosanna

I guess one in the non-smoking section and one in the smoking.

Billy

Then pay for your own fucking tickets!

ii

I used to kid her. I used to tell her not to smoke, for a lot of reasons. It doesn't affect me at all except that I'm sensitive to smoke. It used to affect me, when I was about eleven. I was playing a tennis tournament. I played this kid—I don't remember his name, but I do remember that he had furry eyebrows like an animal and a lisp. I knew I would win from the warm-up, which is usually a bad way to judge. I won the first set, but this eyebrow guy finally realized, in the second set, that I had no backhand. He won the next set, 6-3. Between the second and third sets, we got a break. My mother told me to just win the first game, and I would win. I could tell she was nervous, she was lighting a cigarette. Well, I won the first game, but I lost the second and walked off the court. Actually, I didn't walk anyplace; I couldn't, because it was so hard to breathe. I had to default.

The tournament director, I don't remember his name either, said, "If he's got asthma, he shouldn't play." He might as well have said, 'He's blind, put him away, just get rid of the useless bastard.'

I can assure you that asthma has nothing to do with why I hate Rosanna's smoking. One night about 10:30, we were both working hard. She was designing costumes for a local play—*A Doll's House*, I think. I was writing to the "Fans Speak Out" in *Baseball Digest*, responding to a letter from Mr. Philip Werst of Bloomington, Indiana, who wrote "Day baseball should be abolished." Naturally, this upset me. Baseball is about tradition. Baseball is about blowing off work to go to a game. I want my kids to see a baseball game in the daylight—eating mustardy hot dogs and those chalky little dishes of ice cream that are half-chocolate, half-vanilla, cheering their favorite players, trying to catch foul balls. So I wrote about baseball, and she colored costumes. Every half hour or so, she'd have to use hair spray to protect the pastels from running. The smell of VO-5 hairspray juxtaposed with the smell of the strong, hot coffee we were drinking and the sour, Granny Smith apples we were eating, made it difficult to concentrate. Anyway, we were both working hard at something that seemed terribly important at the time, but in retrospect doesn't seem important at all. We didn't want to take a break, but she ran out of cigarettes. We were both getting pretty hungry, and we didn't want a greasy Domino's pizza. So I called Sol 'n' Sol's Deli to deliver a half pound of chopped liver, a quarter pound of extra-lean corn beef, two Frescas for Rosanna, and a Dr. Brown's black cherry cola for me. She offered to pick up the food (probably, so she could use my car and get cigarettes).

She really wanted a cigarette, even a non-smoker could see that. About a week or so earlier I had bought a pack of cigarettes, just in case. I'm like that. I think ahead. I'm careful.

"What do you wish for, Rosanna?"

"What?" She was getting edgy.

"Close your eyes and make a wish."

I went to the closet and pulled out a pack of Trues. I had bought Trues because they were slightly lower in tar and nicotine, so I could justify it to myself.

"That's what I wished for! I love you. Not because of the cigarettes, but because you think of everything."

I jokingly put a cigarette in my mouth. Normally, a real smoker hates when a non-smoker does that because it wastes a cigarette, but since I bought them, she couldn't complain. She said that she thought I looked sexy, but when I looked in the mirror, I thought I looked ridiculous.

Chapter Seven

When I was twelve years old, I wanted an electric guitar. I wish I was the type of guy who could say, "I saw an old sunburst Les Paul Gibson and I knew I had to have it." But I'm not. I wanted the perfect guitar. It had to have twenty-four frets, so it could reach a high E. It had to have a rosewood body, a maple neck with an ebony fingerboard, gold hardware, and three humbucking pickups. It had to be absolutely perfect.

I walked into Gilsonite music store, the way I did every day, to look at new guitars. I tried to figure out scientific ways of measuring them. I would try to time the response time, the sustain, or other things that were impossible.

The man looked over at me. He was a salesman of medium height, but very fat. Afraid that he would yell at me for not buying anything, I tried to escape his view. I pretended to be looking at the different brands of guitar cleaner, but he spotted me.

"What the hell do you want today, kid?"

"I'm looking for an electric guitar."

"You are?"

"Yes."

"Are you sure?"

"Yes."

"'Cause I don't want to waste my time again."

"No, I'm just looking for the right guitar."

"Do you think that this will be your last guitar?" he

said, as if he knew more. "Why don't you buy one and practice," he said, his cheeks wobbling like jelly. I just stood
there, staring at an old banjo.

"I've got eight guitars at home," he continued. His
overall appearance coupled with his jerky hand movements
disgusted me. Why would anybody want more than one
guitar? How many can you play at once? "He must just buy
them for the hell of it," I thought.

"Well, I just want one." I wish I could tell you that I
stood up to him. But I was twelve years old. I was scared.
I'd only been playing a couple of months, but I practiced a
lot. I began to feel nauseous, an early indication of an ulcer,
I'm told.

I tried out a lot of guitars in that store, and he listened
to me play. What the hell was he trying to say? I started to
shake. I felt I'd eaten too many peanuts. I could throw a
punch at the Great White; I even saw the little bald spot I'd
aim at, but he was too big. "Who the fuck is he?" I thought.
"A guy with eight guitars must be an idiot."

"Stop jerking me off, kid. Either you want to buy one
or you don't."

"Well, I don't want to buy one from you, you fat son of
a bitch," I thought.

I walked out of the store, and I didn't come back until
two and a half years later, when I bought my third guitar.

Chapter Eight

"Get the fuck out of here," I said.

"Why? Because I had to call Hewitt?"

"Yes, and because of when you chose to do it." She chose to do it just as we were getting intimate.

"I chose to do it now because I've blown him off all week."

"You didn't mean anything else by it?" She was clearly saying she didn't want to fool around.

"No."

"Bullshit. You didn't mean anything else by it?"

"No."

"Bullshit. You meant something else by it."

"Well, you go ahead; why don't you tell me what I was thinking." Good technique. She got it from me. Make me justify myself. Make me look like an asshole.

"Get the fuck out of here."

"You want me to leave?"

That's not what I wanted.

"No," I mumbled.

"What?" she licked her upper lip.

"I want to talk."

There are such times. I couldn't leave the wound alone even though I was afraid that I might pick up something. The crap we tell ourselves.

Chapter Nine

i

I do waste my share of time. I spend my time waiting for Rosanna to call, worrying about why she hasn't called, wondering what she's doing, who she's with or if she's thinking about me. I try. I really try. I try to be productive, but when these thoughts... I just can't concentrate.

ii

"I would never say that," she said.

"But you did. You said, 'I thought I loved Hewitt at the time, but maybe I didn't.'"

"That was never in question. Of course I loved him."

I wanted to throw something, but that never helps. And later, it's a bitch to clean up—all those little pieces of glass. Sometimes, they get caught in your skin.

Chapter Ten

i

November's my least favorite month. It's dark all the time and your socks get wet.

In November, Rosanna told me she was going to lunch with Hewitt. Truthfully, it made me sick to think about it. I pictured them in bed together, lying on the floor probably, like dogs. I was supposed to meet her outside J & B's Restaurant. (I'd never eat there because I heard they have rats, but there's a bench outside where I could pick her up.)

She had bought a pair of glasses. She didn't need them, but she liked to wear those rectangular gold-rimmed glasses that looked like prescription glasses.

"Don't wear those," I whined, as she got in the car.

"Why?" she said, in a forgive-me voice, as though she were apologizing for stepping on my toe.

"Because it's perverse to wear glasses if you don't need them."

"I like them."

"I think it's wrong."

"That's convention."

"It's sick to wear glasses if you don't need them."

"You said that before."

Rosanna laughed. Do you know what it's like to be in the world of anger when your partner is in the world of laughter? I started to picture her making love to her ex-boyfriend, Hewitt. I slapped her across the face, but not too hard.

"Don't hit me." She was in my world again. She slapped me back—harder. Hard enough to knock off my glasses.

"You can't hurt me," she said.

"I don't want to hurt you."

"You can't hurt me." And she hit me again.

I turned to punch her arm, but she lifted it to cover her face. I ended up punching her left breast. She mouthed the word "Aoow."

"Now she knows I can hurt her," I thought, and I had a little sympathy.

"Fuck you!" she said.

"No, fuck you." I grabbed both her arms tight.

"You're hurting me!"

"Did you sleep with Hewitt?"

"Yes, and it was great, too."

I let her go.

ii

In June, 1914, a Serbian nationalist assassinated Arch-Duke Francis Ferdinand, heir to the kingdom of Austria-Hungary. This, of course, was the single event that led to World War I.

Chapter Eleven

i

Early one Monday morning I flipped on the TV and there was an aerobics chick, blond, in a tight apricot leotard. I imagined caressing her leg-warmered calves, kissing her breasts as she pumped up and down above me, sweating. Her leotard was so tight I could see everything, even the little mound over her pubis. I imagined all those tight springy curls, lifting the orange fabric. I felt bad. Rosanna woke up.

"What are you watching?"

"Nothing," I said quickly, and switched to the news.

"You were watching that slut."

"Rosanna, don't be like that." I put my hand on her shoulder; she shook it off like a skittish wet dog.

"Put your hand on your penis and think of her. I need a smoke."

ii

"Billy?"

"Yeah."

"Promise me you won't leave me."

"Why? You think I'm going to leave you?"

"I don't know. Don't leave me, Billy."

"I won't."

iii

After we started living together, she and Hewitt...I wish I were a baseball player.

iv

"I do love you, RP," I said, and thought, "Can you ever make someone understand how much you love them?" If you really love someone, then she should be able to see it because it comes out uncontrollably, like diarrhea.

"I love you too, Billy."

If I had a chance to do it all again, I'd change things. I hate when people say, "If I could do it all over, I wouldn't change a thing."

Uncle Louie lost his ring finger in an accident. His first wife was angry or bitchy or careless, I guess, and slammed the car door on his finger. While he was in the hospital, she ran off with a younger man. Every time I saw him he told me, "Billy, no regrets. I found out things about myself I never would have been able to figure out otherwise." He raised his stump as if to surrender; his eyebrows convulsed, and he spoke in a whisper.

I couldn't help but think, "You asshole. You lost your damn finger and your wife. And all that isn't too bad, but you're so goddamned pathetic that you can't admit to yourself that you married a worthless whore and you fucked up your whole life."

But maybe she felt trapped, and had to get out anyway, and what a perfect opportunity with Louie in the hospital. Besides, I knew Louie used to fool around on the side.

Chapter Twelve

i

When I was really young I used to go over to the Faustski's house. Mr. Faustski was a clever man; he had a masculine face and a big gray beard. He liked to laugh and tell stories. "Billy," he said. "I've done many things in this world. I used to drive a truck, I was in the army, I played for a professional baseball team—"

"You did?" I didn't believe him at first, but then it occurred to me that something had to happen to ex-base-ball players.

"Yes I did, but I wouldn't trade this time of my life for anything. I can be with Louise all morning, do a little light gardening, and sit back and collect my retirement. I'm a very happy old man, Billy."

"Tell me about the professional baseball team, Mr. Faustski."

"Sure—I used to play right field for the New Jersey Saints."

"Were you good?"

"Yeah, I guess I was."

"Did you bat fourth?"

"No, I batted leadoff. I remember one game I hit two home runs and made a great running catch."

"Tell me about the home runs."

"Well, I hit two home runs in one game," he repeated.

"Where? Where did you hit them?"

"In Cleveland, I think." He looked confused.

"No, I mean to left field?"

"Yes, to left field."

"Both of them?" Sometimes when you're a kid you need to know everything. I still sometimes push too hard.

"Yeah, both of them." He began to chew on a tooth-pick.

"How far did they go?"

"Oh, I don't remember...way over the fence."

"How far over the fence?"

"I don't remember, Billy."

It seemed sad that he couldn't remember such an important detail. "Come on: try."

"I really don't remember, Billy." He sounded like a teacher. I figured I'd give him one more shot.

"Come on! How far over the fence?"

"I don't know, you lousy kid!" His voice cracked, and the veins on his forehead looked purple, and I guess that scared me, because I ran home and hid.

Eventually, Mrs. Faustski died, and Frank moved in with his brother in Indiana.

ii

I thought I hadn't seen her for a month or so, but I guess I'd lost my sense of time because it'd been almost half a year. Time is funny that way. First it goes too slowly, then it's gone. It's not like I didn't think about her all the time, though. I just kept asking myself hard questions.

Chapter Thirteen

She gave me a washable book. It was some children's book. I knew that I was sweating because my skin started to smell like leather. Something about once you love a toy it's real forever. That's such bullshit.

Chapter Fourteen

I had the day off, so I figured I'd take care of the laundry, the dishes, maybe even clean up. But when I was making scrambled eggs with American cheese, I burned my left thumb. There is little in the world that bothers me more than getting burned. I couldn't concentrate on doing chores; I decided to go guitar shopping.

I wanted to have a real orgy, so I drove out to the place on the highway because they have the biggest selection. The two factors that disturbed me were A) the guitar players there always want to show off, and this is depressing because they are not good—which is a cheat, like the taste of rotten pistachio—and B) the salesmen are often assholes, as you probably know.

The store itself had the bright pink smell of new-guitar. Not the chintzy pink you use for a girl's baby blanket, but the pure, rich strawberry mousse that you get at good French restaurants. The salesmen all had facial hair of some kind. If they get too close, it's annoying because they have stale cigarette breath. Even if they don't smoke themselves (which is rare) they hang out with people who do; it's unavoidable.

It's essential to look like you're a potential buyer or else they won't let you try out the guitars at all. It helps to have a certain kind of uniform—for example, I have a friend who kept his Rutgers graduation robe and then marched in the graduations of two other colleges. I wore a red blazer, a blue button down shirt with a thin suede tie, and faded, torn jeans. I wore Western-style Frye boots that I knew were ten years out of style, but which I figured would eventually come back in. "Excuse me," I said. "I'm interested in purchasing a guitar."

A famished-looking short man looked up—all solicitous, like a reformed gunslinger helping his sweetheart down off the coach at Dodge City. He had short blond hair and a little yellow nicotine smudge at the corner of his mouth. "What are you looking for?"

"I'd like to see a Jackson."

"That's an expensive guitar. You buying today?" He was challenging me, like the cop. But at least the cop wasn't being malicious—he was just doing his job. This guy was looking for a fight, and I was ready to defend my honor.

"American Express okay?" I asked, giving my member-in-good-standing smile.

The guy counted them off on his fingers, like Fagin: "American Express, Visa, and MasterCard."

"I want a guitar with a through-the-body neck."

He brought down an orange Jackson. "By the way," he continued, handing me the guitar. "My name's Paul, what's yours?"

He put out his hand, and I took it, telling him my name. "Here ya go, Billy," he said, plugging the cord in.

You can't feel completely cold to someone who plugs in your guitar—even Asquith might have warmed to the Kaiser if he'd plugged in his guitar. I sat down on an amp, and tuned. I held the neck, but I really didn't notice it, the way you can sometimes forget you have your arm around your girlfriend. I started to play, and the notes sounded like what I had been trying to get out, only I had been constipated. I knew what I was composing: Magnolia's blues.

"Let me see it," Paul said, agitating his fingers.

"What?" He meant the guitar. "Oh, here." I handed him the Jackson.

He played fine, but without distinction. He played from outside, with tricks he'd picked up from others. I recognized them. Eddie Van Headache or something.

"Is there anything else you want to show me?" I asked.

"Yeah, let me think." He kept playing his senseless riffs. Some people play apparently unconnected riffs, but then they come together after a while. Others play fluidly. Paul did neither; his playing was hollow, a bunch of notes circling around something for no reason at all, like Clemente looking for a place to lie down on the floor. To me the best playing has conviction. Otherwise, you're just watching some guy masturbate.

I exhaled, to let him know I was getting bored.

"Maybe a Paul Reed Smith," he said, as if all this time he'd been thinking it over. He put the Jackson away. I realized I felt less attractive without Rosanna; even when we weren't together, it felt sexy knowing she loved me. "These are handmade in Maryland," he added.

My thumb hurt, so I started to play, because when I did the burn didn't bother me as much.

"Let me check it out," said Paul. He added a chorus effect to round out the sound, make it prettier. But it was still gibberish.

I let him go on even longer this time. Finally I spoke up. "They're both beautiful. I'm going to have to think about it overnight."

"When you thinking of buying?"

"I'm going out of town at the end of the week, so I'll have to pick it up soon."

"Which one you thinking of?"

"Let me sleep on it."

He perked up. "Well, why don't you leave a deposit on one?"

"Why?" I noticed a piece of scrambled egg in his oily beard, just a small scrap of yellow.

He shrugged. "Otherwise, someone comes in and starts

lookin' at it, I can't tell him some other guy might want that. It really puts me in a bad spot. If you leave a small deposit on it, I can save it for you."

"How much?" I was teasing him.

"I don't know. Fifty, sixty bucks."

"Paul, if you can sell it, definitely do it."

"And so I know you're not playing with me."

I wasn't going to spend fifty bucks to prove I was serious. I held back, and calmly explained, "Paul." If you call someone by their name, take a pause, it's always effective. "I'm spending over a thousand bucks. I really don't need anyone putting pressure on me."

"I'm not putting pressure on you." He backed down. He was like a child whose Mother had yelled at him. "Paul, don't you dare put pressure on that nice young man."

I noticed a beautiful tobacco sunburst Jackson. "What about that? How much is that?"

He looked. "That one has killer wood. It's twelve hundred, but some guy has a hold on it."

"How long is that good for?"

He perked up again. "A small deposit? About a week."

I began to think about making an offer for it just to see what he'd do. I was pretty sure he would sell. Then I'd say, "You fucking cheat. Get me an honest guy."

"Want to check it out?" Paul asked.

"Sure."

He took it down, and I noticed a tag that said HOLD. It said "M. Anthony" and it had two phone numbers.

"Check out this grain," he said. "It matches. See?"

It really was pretty, but I didn't want someone else's axe. I thought about making Paul call the guy up, to see if he would release the hold, but I realized that that wouldn't do anything. I already knew Paul wasn't afraid to put the pressure on, and I really didn't want this guy's guitar. At least, not badly enough to put that rotten pistachio taste in someone else's mouth.

"Maybe I'll come back before the end of the week, Paul."

I squeezed out a smile and left quietly. When I put my hand in my pocket to get my car keys, I felt the burn on my thumb.

Chapter Fifteen

"Billy, do you like me?" was running through my head.

I don't know anymore. I start thinking about Uncle Louie and his wife. But don't get the wrong idea. This is my problem. Poor Rosanna had nothing to do with this. But to picture her with that cockroach Hewitt. I had a chance to beat the shit out of him. Oh, Lord, give me that chance back. Don't turn me into Louie the mouse.

It was in a bar. I don't remember the name of it, but it was one of those grimy places where your shoes stick to the floor. It's the kind of a bar that you would never go to, but you always have one friend who insists it is the coolest bar, and you always let her talk you into coming along.

I saw her with Hewitt there that night. I honestly didn't notice Rosanna at first, but I'm sure she saw me because, when I did finally notice her, she was talking like they do in a Daffy Duck cartoon. It's funny when you realize how much concentration it takes to pretend you don't see somebody.

I was with Robin, Rosanna's best friend. I was upset and I wanted to be with a woman. Just as friends. The hell with it; the truth is I was fucking crying. I didn't know what to do, but I didn't want to be alone.

Robin made me promise that I wouldn't hit Hewitt. She said, "When you get the urge to hit him, just hold onto it, for me. Okay, Billy? You can't go around getting into bar-room brawls."

I didn't see the connection, but Robin was enthusiastic, so I laughed one of those uncomfortable laughs.

Rosanna pretended to be very friendly as she talked to Robin, and later I found out she was a little worried about Robin and me. But when I spotted Hewitt he was fading away like a little television dot, so there was no first punch at all.

Chapter Sixteen

I could recognize her by her footsteps. It sounded like opening roasted peanuts, delicate and deliberate. I pictured her hips shaking as she walked up the stairs; she really has a beautiful walk.

The bed was messy with stains of blood and mucus. But it wasn't dirty; at least it didn't feel that way to me. The pillowcase was supposed to be orange, but tonight it looked distinctly yellowish, like the two-week-old *New York Times* Sports section still in the back seat of my white Cutlass.

I was tired, but I just couldn't sleep. I wanted to sleep; I tried to relax myself by escaping into the world of "I walk into that bar and pull a Bruce Lee on Hewitt," but this got my adrenaline flowing and only made sleep harder. I tried the world of "I'll show you, you no-good slut," but that didn't work. Then I thought I'm Richard III and I got what I wanted, though in the end Richard dies.

Finally, I imagined that I was the starting second baseman for the Dodgers and I had to get a hit off Gooden.

Chapter Seventeen

i

Mitchell Spitzer's father was always involved in little league, so I really got to know him well. I saw that movie about the kids who played organized baseball versus the kids who played in a playground. It was trying to show how children use their imaginations and learn to get along better without adults. I don't agree. I think you can learn from watching what people do in organized situations.

Besides, that film didn't tell you about Mr. Spitzer, our little league coach, taking us out to the Royal Palm Diner for spaghetti and cheeseburgers. He taught us how to order politely from waiters, and he taught us to throw straight and hit to all fields, so I respected him. He was the first person except for Matty that I felt that about and the first of my friends' fathers that I really liked. And I loved that baseball field, home plate shining like a tooth.

It was the type of day where the sky looks like watermelon Italian Ice. Mr. Spitzer was showing us how to step out with his left foot. "If he throws you that low inside fastball, pull it down the line. I guarantee a double every time. But," he lit a Lucky, "it's not easy to bend from the knees and drive that ball. You need good wrist-snap, too."

Mrs. Spitzer made kosher hot dogs with sauerkraut and coleslaw, and cold orange drink. Mitchell was the last of my friends to be allowed to watch R-rated movies, so I was especially surprised when Mitchell's mom invited me to go to the movies to see *Ten*. After the movie we waited for

Mrs. Spitzer to use the ladies' room.

Mitchell's father inhaled another Lucky, "You know what that movie shows you?" In fact, I was just thinking that it was stupid to have a movie about a guy who wants a meaningful relationship instead of a superficial one; that's like having a choice between a Lancia that doesn't run or a Cutlass that works. Mr. Spitzer paused to let us wonder. "That movie shows you that the grass is always greener." I didn't agree, but I realized that I should just shut up and respect him.

I thought about what Mr. Spitzer said for a long time and decided that he must have had an affair, but afterwards he knew he made a mistake and went back to his wife.

ii

What was that Beatles song? "And in the end/the love you take/is equal to the love you make." Must have been written by Paul because that's just wishful thinking.

iii

Matty worked for my Dad, but he was a great guy. We played stickball, when he wasn't busy. Matty was twenty. He went to Rutgers because it was a state school. "Billy the Kid!" He called me that; I took it as a compliment. "I got my first house. It's big." Matty and five other guys had rented a house.

"Wow." Big is a key word for a kid. I started picturing Jeffersonian mansions—white columns and wisteria hanging down. I don't even think they have those in New Jersey.

"You have to come over for Sloppy Joes."

I couldn't believe what a dump it was. I grew up in pretty much a Brady Bunch neighborhood, and I just wasn't accustomed to old houses where paint is chipping because they forget to strip beforehand.

"Do you like it? It's great, isn't it." He was so enthusiastic.

"Yes it is," I said, letting the words fall dependably and rhythmically, like a laundry machine.

iv

There is no question that I made a mistake when I stopped speaking to Rosanna.

Chapter Eighteen

i

I know it was stupid for Marie Antoinette to say, "Let them eat cake." But don't you feel sorry for her? She didn't know it was wrong and, besides, she shouldn't have been beheaded for that. Who knows, maybe the French had some special cake that was like bread but it was cheap and easy to make. Maybe the whole thing was a mistake. I bet she was sweet.

ii

Rosanna and I took long drives up to upstate New York. When you work as a production assistant, you get time off and you need it. I don't want to get into it, but you have to do all the shit work, which isn't so bad. The bad thing is when you don't get respect. If I had been a building custodian, at least the people who lived there would be nice. You know, they would smile and say, "Hey Billy. How ya doing?" In the film business you have to have something to offer. I don't know how to explain it. Everybody's thinking, "What can *you* do for me?" etc. What those people don't realize is that every job is important. The best people in that business are the ones who don't let it get to their heads. Like if I'm the guy who's responsible for the trash, then I think it's nice if people respect that and get the garbage into the bags. I know I always do. It makes things suck if you have to clean the pails. To just tie up bags and throw them out is no big deal, but that vomit-like smell of rotten food...it just makes things unpleasant and you feel bad about other things, too. Even the smell's not so bad if the people you're working with still respect you. So I try not to work too often, and Rosanna had time off, too, so we'd drive upstate just for the peace. She said that the trees looked like broccoli.

iii

It felt so good to drive and be in love and not even talk. Sometimes we'd listen to local radio stations or a funky tape (we both love funky guitar). Sometimes we'd listen to nothing, just the engine or the wind or something. A lot of times we didn't eat, so when we got to a town we'd get a slice of pizza or McDonald's or maybe we'd walk around and buy a soda or walk through a bakery. The key thing was staying pretty much outside, so sit-down places were out. But after a while of eating fast food you really can't do it. You'd rather be hungry.

So we were walking around some nice town that claimed to be the home of Mark Twain, which of course is ridiculous but harmless, and we walked through a bakery. It was a mother and her daughter. We started to look at the birthday cakes, even though it was nobody's birthday. Rosanna was only interested in the ones with white cake; I guess they seemed more happy, and even though I prefer almost anything to be chocolate, I really did agree. Besides I like to have a rule that helps me decide. You know like if you have that same jacket in pink, I'll buy it. It's one of those things that sounds insane, but works.

We looked at the cakes in the display case. There were two that the mother said had white cake. One was pink and one was yellow. I said we should take the yellow, and we did. She asked us if we wanted anything written on it.

"We love you, Magnolia," Rosanna said.

We ate the cake with two forks, no slices. We just dug in. We ate it over a day and a half instead of real food.

Chapter Nineteen

i

I spent one afternoon alone. There was a book and record fair at the mall. There I bought a used copy of *Coriolanus*. It was so old that the first six letters were worn away. It was one of those purchases where you know you'll probably never even look at it, but for three bucks you have to own it.

I bought a glass of white wine from a blonde woman with a child. She smelled like Charmin or baby powder or diapers. The wine was too sharp, and I told her so. She let me try another for free. An old black man with a fat moustache came over. He asked to look at the wines. He knew what he was doing. He shook the wine to check for sediment. Before purchasing the red wine, he'd want to taste it. It made sense, but she was reluctant. She treated him like a wino, but he knew what he was doing. It's good, he told me. I had a glass. He sat down. I paid and asked him if I could join him. No resentment at all. Prejudice, I screamed. Yes, he said, but they are now on the defensive. Muslim, he was. It was the black son who laughed at his father who was naked and drunk. Where did I learn that? He knew where. Hebrew school. Lie to children.

You do what you gotta do, he said.

ii

Rosanna and I were on our way out the door. As we

hurried to my car, it began to rain, so I covered her with my newspaper. It took fifteen minutes to get to the car, which I had parked sixteen blocks away to avoid a ticket (I could never figure out that odd/even parking, so I left the car on a side street). She was wet, and her makeup was running. Strangely, however, she looked great. During that walk we talked about everything; we speculated about the future, and we planned. We decided to spend as little time apart as we could; we told each other how happy we were, dreaming and talking of the future. We felt lucky. She wanted to support herself by becoming a real costume designer, and still have a family of three kids. Believe it or not, that sounded good to me. I think it was because she already loved her children passionately, and even though they were not born yet, she knew what they would feel like in her arms, and how they would cry when they skinned a knee, and how they would laugh and play on Christmas. We loved to see children play; it seemed to make her happy just to see them, and it was contagious. I began to dream about directing my own films or at least becoming a production manager. I'd need a lot of money for the children; I wanted to spoil them to death, and give them all the advantages. We would travel to Europe and speak French. I don't know how to speak French, but I could learn and teach the children. We would travel across the countryside by train, preferring to avoid those sub-compact cars, not to mention the European drivers. We would have two girls and a boy. The children wouldn't have to dance and sing or be athletes or doctors or artists, unless they wanted to do those things, and that would be okay, too. Because the important thing is that everybody would feel love all around them; it would be real. Like strawberry rhubarb pie, you could taste it. We would all get up early Sunday morning and watch cartoons in our bedroom. Everyone would climb on the bed, except of course the puppy because I'm allergic. But he could sleep late in the barn, if we bought a house in the country. We wouldn't farm, because I've always been afraid of farm accidents, especially to children, but we would have a barn just for fun. And Rosanna, the kids, and I would grow old and be happy, I guess. I just hope I like their friends.

iii

I didn't have this problem. With few exceptions, my parents liked my friends. And, in fact, the problems that they had with those few friends that they didn't like were about fifty-eight per cent valid. I mean valid fifty-eight per cent of the time. They didn't like my friend Bobby, but I learned a lot from him. I mean he fucked up himself, but he had some good ideas.

Mostly he was fast; he could outrun you.

Chapter Twenty

i

"**Y**ou mean you're not coming home?" I could smell my bad breath on the phone.

"I don't know," Rosanna said softly, like a cotton ball.

"You mean you *might* not come home?" I could feel my back curling over like a deformed dwarf, but my muscles felt too weak to straighten out.

"I don't know. We're talking. We might talk for a while." She was at Hewitt's house.

"Well, I'm gonna be up late playing so I don't care if you come home late." I knew I wouldn't be able to sleep without putting my arms around her stomach and hearing her breathe.

"Well, I might just spend the night." This was very bad news.

"What does that mean?"

"Look Billy, I haven't seen Hewitt in months and I might spend the night." There was a moment of silence. "If we stay up talking...we haven't spoken. We have a lot to talk about."

"I'm not opposed to talking." I just didn't want him to put his arm around her naked belly.

"Look, he's worried about me."

"So am I."

"He thinks you might be dangerous."

"I might be." I had to keep her scared. If she thought I was dangerous, maybe she'd be too scared to fuck around.

"He told my parents that you might be dangerous to me. Now, everybody is panicked. My parents want it straightened out tonight."

"Then I'd better come over. I'll talk to both your parents." Here I come to save the day.

"No. I told them that the three of us got together and talked it out."

"That's a lie." I'd lost her. "I might be dangerous."

"I know."

"I'm going to come by. This is bullshit. I want to talk to you in person."

"No." She wasn't going to be bullied anymore.

"Why?"

"I told you we haven't seen each other in a long time and we need to talk."

"I'm coming by."

"Don't."

"Okay, but I'm gonna put all your stuff in boxes and leave them in the hall. You can pick them up anytime you want." She once told me how upsetting it was when Hewitt did that to her, so I knew it was a weak spot. But it was also a cheap thing to do, and I felt bad about it later. It wasn't even my idea.

"Don't put my stuff in boxes."

"I'm gonna come by, then."

"Okay, but just honk the horn." She hung up on me.

I was really hungry.

ii

Obviously, I thought that if I could talk to her in person, I could get her to come home. She wanted everything. I wanted her, but she remained elusive like music.

iii

"Our love was like the water/that splashes on a stone. Our love is like our music/It's here and then it's gone." I played "No Expectations" by the Stones. It has that heavy slide guitar that I wanted to hear before I went over. Those old blues guys got that sound by pressing a knife against the strings. Traditionally, it's supposed to sound like someone's soul screaming or something. It's the way the knife on the strings cuts through that mushy blues progression and that rainy sound that those single high acoustic piano notes make that pushes the forceful slide through the marshmallow rain.

iv

My appetite evaporated, and I pulled on a gray sweatshirt. I went down the elevator that I had once stopped so that we could have sex, and I plopped into my white Cutlass.

v

I parked the car and rang the front bell. Rosanna put her finger up. "I'll be out in a minute," she said.

She came out and closed the door. She was wearing a jacket and she had an unlit cigarette in her hand, like she was taking a coffee break.

"Hi," I said like a kid who's been mischievous.

"What do you want, Billy?" She lit up.

"What's going on? I love you."

"I love you, too." She inhaled. "Don't throw my stuff out in the hall, Billy."

"I'm going to do it." I couldn't believe myself. I was begging her to come with me.

"What's wrong?"

"What do you think is wrong?" She knew.

"Look, we haven't seen each other in a long time and we just want to talk."

"Oh." I acted sincere. "...Talk?"

"Yes." She hit it hard.

"So will you come home tonight?"

"Maybe."

For a second I thought she might. Besides, I had no choice. "Give me a kiss," I said, like a prisoner's last request.

She kissed me, and laughed sharply. Then she looked at me very seriously the way a mother looks at her child. "Now don't throw my stuff into the hall."

I stayed up all night and got really fucked up so that I would be well prepared for the hard day ahead.

vi

The first time I stayed up all night was when I was a kid. I'd heard some guy on the radio talking about these predictions. When he got to the year two thousand he said it was supposed to be the end, no more life. All my family and friends would be dead. I'd begun to think about mortality, and I ran up and down the stairs for a while, but it was useless. On the radio there was a guy who once said that if you stay up all night you can sometimes cure a depression.

I stayed up in my room, and then I walked into the kitchen to lie in the fluorescent light. I stared at the clock. Mostly I just sat there trying to see the different colors in the light, just not sleeping. I didn't even want to. Then, as the natural light overcame the fluorescent light, I felt better.

vii

The Spitzers laughed when I told them I was depressed. Kids aren't supposed to act that way.

Chapter Twenty-One

"**B**illy?" she said.

"Yeah." It was Sunday and I was reading the Sports section (it has really good trade gossip about baseball).

"Hi," she said.

"Hi." I held up my hand to indicate major concentration.

"Billy, do you love me?"

"Yes, of course." And that's the problem. You don't love someone "of course." I should have held her and kissed her fingertips and pulled her close and touched her shoulder. I should have made her feel the way you do when you eat home-baked apple pie with cinnamon on Thanksgiving. Or the way you feel when you camp out in the woods and see the sun peep out from behind the hills. The bright yellow colors that make the rich green hills look brown at sunrise as opposed to the cool purple of the sunset. That's what I should have done when Rosanna asked me if I still loved her. I should have taken her outside to some beautiful place. She hugged me.

"I'm reading," I said. Scrooge.

I went for a walk, just to get out—to think. I walked by a little pond, and looked up at the moon. I was alone, so I even cried a little. But it was strange: in order to make myself cry, I had to tell myself that she'd never loved me, which I knew wasn't true. I picked up a flat rock, trying to make it skim the water. I threw out my arm.

Chapter Twenty-Two

She kissed my neck and I felt her breath on me like a red wool Christmas glove and then she lowered her mouth to my chest and as she slithered back, my neck felt cold. I circled her aureola with my tongue and held her nipple between my teeth. Reaching down I caressed her bottom, and I massaged her upper thigh then her hairy crack. The completeness of being in love. Something that I had never understood, and not the way I didn't understand Caesar. It was much more like the way you play baseball and you keep missing the ball. You can't hit a curve and, all of a sudden, you learn how to wait and you can guard the plate. Or the way that you play a cello and in just that way the way the cello plays you and the hopelessness of not being able to finish your piece evaporates. It's the opposite of failing to concentrate because you're drunk or inadequate, I guess. Anyway, it was amazing.

Chapter Twenty-Three

i

It's amazing what people throw away. I mean I guess I threw away a lot of stuff that I shouldn't have. Sometimes, when I go drop off film at the lab, I'll ask for some extra junk footage so I can practice editing. I get a lot of outtakes from commercials, you know, Chevrolet or Life Cereal or Pepsi. Anyway, I have a little editing rig at home, and one day Ross came by. Ross and I went to high school together, but I hardly ever see him because he works mostly in Japan, so I was pretty surprised. He sells American music to clubs over there for their jukeboxes. Now he's getting into video jukeboxes. He said that he just takes footage of landscapes and puts instrumental music to it. He said that he gets all this music from artists who are doing badly over here and need the money. He says that they even get followings in Japan. The point is, he said we'd make some money if he could use the crap that I'd been editing. I thought we might get in trouble with Pepsi, but he said we should take the chance. Pepsi has better things to do. He said the chance of anything bad happening was obscure. Besides, they threw the stuff in the trash anyway. Once something gets thrown away you lose the rights anyway, he said. I needed the money.

ii

I can't throw out letters. When she moved, she brought

the letters that I wrote her, too. So now I can't throw out those letters either.

iii

The first time she went back to Hewitt sucked, but I knew she couldn't drop me like that and it was easy to get back. Well, easier than impossible, which is what it is now. I tried to put her out of my mind, you know, become pre-occupied with something else, but I wasted my time. She could be engaged or something. Even if she's not engaged, I'm worried that she's not thinking of me. But of course she's thinking about me. I want to see her more than anything, and I would give up my stupid demands, too.

iv

I thought of Rosanna as a car that you run into the ground and then trade in.

v

I keep eating these Hostess pudding pies. They taste really sweet, but you know you're just eating junk food. It's so depressing to have those sticky wrappers in your garbage pail.

Chapter Twenty-Four

I met someone new, but it took me five years. Her hair was a fresh brewed cup of coffee on a fall day. The coffee has a faint smell of cinnamon. The wind is crisp, and it almost burns your nose, so you need something hot—that is her pained look of trying to follow what you are saying.

"So, how long do you know each other?" I ask. But instead of listening carefully I am falling in love. Not the sinking feeling, and maybe I'm wrong about the whole thing. But, it makes me feel good to talk to her—she is charming. I love the way she holds her wine glass. It rests gently in her hand like a sleeping kitten. It's been three years since Rosanna, I realize.

She touches my forehead to make a joke. I am like a high-school kid. I hope she doesn't notice my acne, I think. The club is dark; it is late. She won't notice.

This is Manhattan—with all of its *natural* trash—I am ready to roll away the tears.

Chapter Twenty-Five

My friend, Lester, laughs as I tell him I am in love.

"Hey, Billy, maybe you're a lonely man who's in the middle of something that he doesn't really understand."

"Yeah, and yesterday came suddenly."

"All I'm saying is you jump into things too quickly. Did you get her number?"

"Of course." I have made the mistake of giving out my number, but you never get called. I guarantee you'll never get called unless it's a fluke.

"And her name is—?" he asks.

I do not know her last name. "Jean-Maria."

"You have any beer?"

Chapter Twenty-Six

I wanted to kiss her, you know—a real kiss. So rather than give her a peck or touch her even, I did nothing. I like to think I built the tension.

Chapter Twenty-Seven

"I felt like I was in a tailspin," I tell my therapist, and I can't imagine how you would ever fall in love with your shrink. "I mean, for three years I was climbing out of this giant barrel filled with olive oil, and I was like a cowboy grabbing at the sides, getting captured by Indians—all the things you use to see on *F-Troup*. Finally, I stick my head out, and I have a new point of view."

"That's wonderful," she says like espresso ice cream—a stronger flavor than plain coffee.

Chapter Twenty-Eight

i

John Lennon took five years away from making records. Then he exploded, and recorded *Starting Over*. He released it, and then he was shot.

ii

Rosanna had been gone for four years before I could get out of that tailspin. When I was a kid, I had the perception my friends at school, my parents and the Mets were the world. Rosanna was all three, at one point. You worry so much sometimes.

Every year when the Mets' season started there was hope. And every year they lost, the next year seemed like a long time away.

iii

Starting over is a lot like dying.

Chapter Twenty-Nine

i

When the people in the *Wizard of Oz* are living in black and white, do they realize it?

ii

I got a call from an old college friend, Joe, to play opposite Bugs Bunny in some promos for ABC. There was a young woman who asked me to help her zip her dress. Actors are like that—craving attention. They'll have no trouble getting dressed in front of the opposite sex. That's how you get to be an actor. You have to be an exhibitionist at heart.

"I'm playing Dorothy from the *Wizard of Oz*." She looked like she was about fifteen. I felt uncomfortable touching her in just a slip.

"Wasn't Dorothy a speed freak in real life?"

"What?" She smiled like she was my secretary and I had just asked her to take dictation. It's a chore, but that's what I'm here for.

"Are you still in school?"

"No I dropped out."

"Really!" I was surprised.

"Yeah, well I was studying marketing so it was pretty useless. I'm working a lot."

"Wow, you were in college."

"Yeah," she lit a smoke.

"I thought you were much younger." I was relieved. I realized that I was wearing a pretty strange costume—real trippy: tie-dye, a *Clockwork Orange* hat and a vest.

"How old?"

"Eighteen, nineteen." I didn't want to be too far off.

"I'm twenty-three." Then she pulled out a book of *Contemporary American Short Stories* that had a lot of Edgar Allen Poe.

I figured she had a lot of catching up to do, so I better let her read on.

Chapter Thirty

i

She wore a nose ring and had dreadlocks; her earrings had big Jewish stars. It gave me a weird feeling that I couldn't control. It's like the way onions make you cry every time, but you think this time they won't.

ii

"Sit anywhere you like?" she said in a friendly Brooklyn accent, like a Saint Bernard with a flask of Peppermint Schnapps.

"Woody Allen is the best student filmmaker in the country," said Bobby. His conversation was elevator music.

"You want a beer?" I asked, but I was thinking about a shot of Jack.

"Beer and a shot of Vodka," Bobby ripped-back like a fast typist.

As I got up to get the first round, I noticed the hostess again. She had all kinds of chains on (not the big gold stuff)—cheap, thin silver chains some looked like dogtags, but they had different symbols. I couldn't figure out what they said from the distance. It didn't have anything to do with glasses. It was just far away. Anyway, they formed a line down her chest. The way the mirrors were set up in that place, I realized, I could see the hostess chick very clearly. I suddenly felt she was beautiful. She used her energy to heat herself up from inside, like a sweet potato when it gets all juicy. It's an unmistakable smell that fills the room.

Maybe I'd misjudged one thing with Rosanna. If I'd misjudged one small thing, like the faint notion that love is a rock, then in a way I'd misjudged everything. I should have left Rosanna alone a long time ago. She became my mysterious secret that separated me from the world. I'd been thrown out like trash, or maybe I treated her like trash.

She's the shadow or maybe a strange reflection in a puddle in the street—she's the gold in the yellow part of the rainbow. The gold, which more famous fools have chased, is the taste of a sweet orange, the smell of its skin where the oil is, and the juicy nectar that the Tropicana people would love to sell you. They throw out the skin of the oranges anyway, sacrificing the smell in order to sell the juice.

Gold is worthless—I realized that. It's all pyrite. Fool's gold.

iii

I sold my car. I was tempted to get sentimental, but instead I got a garlic bagel.

Chapter Thirty-One

i

My mother kissed my ear in a way that sucked the life out of me. The sound made me close my eyes. It was like Rosanna with a Marlb light. Made me think of Oedipus.

ii

My mother has strawberry blonde hair.

iii

I just thought I should make mention of my mother, in case you were curious.

iv

"Billy!" she would sing in two octaves. "Billy, time to walk the dogs." We had two English cocker spaniels (that I was allergic to), and I had to walk the dogs, but it was always done in a harsh voice—like someone smacking you hard in the head. My back stiffened.

Chapter Thirty-Two

i

I've got a shark in my brain.

ii

I stopped eating fish altogether. I know it's supposed to be good luck, but that's a lot of crap. Besides, I don't know anyone who likes the smell.

iii

"Billy," said Rosanna. "What do you think we would talk about if we were dolphins?"

"Do dolphins talk?" I said, pulling my green sweater out of the closet. I was hustling to get some shopping done before work in the afternoon.

"Sure they do," she grabbed the extra blanket from the foot of the bed, trying to extend the morning.

"We'd probably sing."

"I like that, Billy. Kiss me."

iv

Myer, the production coordinator, left a message on the machine. "Hey Billy, we need you to help Dorothy with lunch. So it's very important that you pick up the van at ten."

I called him back at the production office.

"She's bringing a special vegetarian thing with fish, so help her carry everything."

"Myer, fish isn't vegetarian."

He coughed into the phone, clearing his throat of mucus. "I don't give a fuck what it is. You just have to pick the fucking van up and help the damn woman with it."

"I just mean that you can't serve it to vegetarians."

"Dude, don't you have enough to worry about without this fish shit? I know I do, and I don't have time. Come on now. Get a fucking move-on."

"I don't want to think about fish either."

Chapter Thirty-Three

I was going to meet Bobby and Jack. It was my first time at this bar in Tribeca called The Trip. It was a super-hip, Grateful Dead, yuppie crowd. Rich kids mostly. A strange group of people came in the bar, an old woman with a cane, and then an old man, and then two or three old women. They were all together. Jack said they looked like they were into witchcraft. We took the chance and got high right there anyway. And, Jack ordered shots of gin.

"Gin shots. You're out of your fucking mind," said the waitress as she left us to contemplate our future.

"I love the miniskirt," said Bobby.

"Thanks," she said leaving.

"Why do you do that?" I said.

"Do what?" said Bobby.

"You are an asshole, Bob."

"What's the fuck's wrong with you?" Jack interrupted.

"He's practically jerking off in the bar. It's embarrass-ing." I said, overreacting. But you would, too, if you had to work for that fucking Myer character for a month.

I didn't even notice that the old woman with the cane had dropped the cane, walked over to me and was about to ask a question. I figured she wanted to know the time or where the bathroom was.

"Will you join us for a drink?" she asked me.

I thought maybe she was into witchcraft after all, and I wasn't afraid.

"Sure," I said.

As I escorted her to her table, she asked me what I do.

"I'm in the film business. No make that garbage."

"Oh, we have friends in both industries."

"Oh, really who?" I said trying to be an opportunist. I noticed her wrinkles and Grateful Dead-type paisley skirt. She had to have been in her sixties.

"Do you dance?" she squeaked.

"Do you?" I said like ping-pong.

"Yes, I love to dance." She sung the word yes like a broken-down hooker might, if you slipped her a twenty. The question, obviously, had been a mistake, a trap I fell into gracefully like a ballerina on toe.

"Here, take this number," she continued. "We do yoga, and have a party."

"Why would you invite me?" Her friend put her hand on my lap. I looked at her hard, but not daring her, more like making fun of her predicament. She was a moth about to be crushed into a paper napkin. She retreated.

"Because you're cute," said the woman with the cane, giggling like little girl. "Here," she said getting up without her cane. "Come with me."

I went to confront her witchcraft and destroy her belief in the devil, but I guess I was projecting.

"Call this number," she said like Helen Hayes on acid. "It's fun. There's lots of pretty boys and girls," she said implying a huge bisexual orgy—something Roman. "I bet you could use some investors. I invested in this young, doctor student. I have to see him later." Double bubble toil and trouble. I felt sorry for the warrior Macbeth, took the number and hurried back to my gin.

Chapter Thirty-Four

i

All kids want to pitch in little league. The fantasy was a heroic pitching performance in the important game. It was easy, and this was my chance. I was known as a control pitcher. The orange sky looked like those ice bars from the Good Humor man. This was big; even my father attended this game. In fact it was the only game he ever attended.

I was Tom Seaver. I hit the first kid with a pitch, a younger boy, and I felt bad. I walked over to apologize, but you don't do that in little league. I couldn't pitch strikes because all I could think about was that I was onstage. A poor player to be sure. Walking in all those runs. I couldn't see the catcher's mitt quite, and I just felt outside myself.

I was asking a lot of questions about death and nobody (my father) wanted to answer me. I read a book about American Indians saying that they honored their dead symbolically by burying the heart of a buffalo. The minerals in the heart actually replenish the earth. It feeds the tree of life, knowledge, etc. My fear of death had diminished the quality of my game. Every kid's fantasy tastes like a stick of bubble gum, the kind you get in baseball card packs. The stick used to be the size of a card.

I sat on the bench as the orange in the sky turned purple. I was by myself.

ii

Is Willy Loman an old Indian chief with great wisdom,
or is he some Dustin Hoffman guy with a chick in Boston,
say? His sales pitch stopped working, and he had no control. Rejected and alone, maybe even obsessed with death,
he created it like a Jackson Pollock painting.

iii

Rejected and alone with a true sense of perfectionism,
Pollock, unable to complete the game...

Chapter Thirty-Five

In this dream I decided to sneak back over to Hewitt's house. I figured even if I got caught, there was no way anybody would do anything to me. What would Hewitt do, hold me down until the police arrived? Besides, I wasn't going to get caught. I drove by the house five times. Finally, I parked on a side road next to an alley, so that I could make a quick escape into my Cutlass, if I had to. I pictured Rosanna like a chewed up piece of gum. In this fantasy, she was being held down by this evil Hewitt. I dive into the house through the window and come up punching. Hewitt looks scared, and I'm wearing a Mets uniform.

Chapter Thirty-Six

i

The pigeons mock me as they fly. My first novel came to me one day.

ii

A friend of mine, Nicky, who is getting her master's at Hopkins was in town, and she, remembering me (in a way that reminded me of Hamlet remembering his old man), bought tickets for Ubu Roi at Lincoln Center. I offered to pay on the phone.

"You've taken me to so many shows." She'd remembered me from my wealthy days. Her voice was homemade chocolate pudding still hot with the dark skin on top. Sweet, but kind of sloppy. "I'll meet you at one in front." She hung up quickly.

I knew we both had different ideas about what "in front" meant. But sometimes you can't call back.

I positioned myself, in the sun, from a point at which I could view two entrances at once. Plus, there was an attractive, and I admit slightly young-looking woman to my left, who I later found out was with her parents who were just ten feet down from her. Enough distance to convince me that she was alone. I don't know what I was thinking.

I still didn't see Nicky. I figured I could circle around, like the dog I told you about, make my circle smaller and eventually I would find her. It wouldn't have worked because as it worked out we did have totally different ideas about what "in front" meant. I almost did it but my parents taught me to stay in one place and let them find you. In this case, we both stayed where we were and so nothing happened until ten to two when we met in the theatre.

The play was cool. This guy, Jarry, made fun of his high school teacher and it became a play. A hundred years ago there were riots because of the offensive language. The king's first word is shit. Actually, it's not even the whole word, but just the implication that when the king wakes up the first thing he says is shit. A hundred years ago, that made people crazy. But when people walked out of the play on a cold Saturday in 1989, it didn't make sense to me. They were still offended? I know: new people. But, if you're going to pay thirty bucks for a show in New York, you should at least have some vague idea of what is going on. In fact, even if you're not paying anything.

When the playwright died at thirty-four, Jarry's last request was for a toothpick. Not a good sign.

iii

Chuck Berry and Elvis should do a concert together. Elvis is the King. Let's say he's King of England, that would make Chuck Berry, and T-Bone Walker before him, what? And, let's not forget the original "Hound Dog" was actually written by Big Mama Thorton, what would Churchill say? I'm sure he's had experience in these matters. I wonder what his voice would sound like musically—his diction and grammar like a tuba. It's a whole different style. That is one thing. This is another: Elvis put his name on something he didn't write, and not a high-school paper, but a rich man stealing from a person who needed the cash. I'm talking about the fact that the song existed, was recorded, and was a hit before The King decided he wrote it. The King might be fat.

iv

Elvis had a twin that died in childbirth. It's a well-known fact. Elvis and Churchill were twins, most likely.

v

And before Bo Diddley it was a Native American beat.

vi

I had an interview with RCA Records on Thursday, and my friend's wedding was on Saturday. I was deciding if I should wear a blue shirt or a white shirt. One decision—which shirt I should wear to the interview—would solve both problems.

vii

Elvis died on the toilet, you know. That's just not a good sign. RCA, however, had such a favorable deal that the Elvis catalogue kept them afloat for decades. I guess The King is still the king even after he dies.

viii

I wonder if Rosanna still has red hair.

ix

I'm not a guy who still listens to 45s, but I found this old child's portable record player in the trash, when I was with Rosanna. It must have been a decade ago (or a moment, it really doesn't matter). It's the kind that has a cover that you lift off and it becomes the speaker—the kind you had as a kid. Anyway, it had an old Elvis record in it so

I grabbed it as a joke.

My bed is just a king size mattress on the floor—it takes up most of the room. So, for years the record player stared at me from across the floor. Finally, I was going to throw it out because it started playing weird games with my mind, like Rosanna was staring at me.

I keep batteries of every size in my refrigerator—not a lot of them, but at least three or four of each major size. I like to anticipate moments sometimes. I love the excitement of dropping a fresh set of batteries into an old flashlight you suddenly need. Anyway, just for kicks I popped in four C Duracells.

The B side, "Any Day Now," had been scratched pretty badly, so I flipped it over. It worked! I smiled as I heard the crackling of an old 45 coming through the one toy speaker. Hearing Elvis sing "In the Ghetto" was like a fresh banana when you are really hungry.

For a second I could smell Elvis frying up bananas for peanut butter sandwiches. I like my bananas ripe, but still completely yellow (if possible). I walked into the kitchen and grabbed one that had a few brown spots. It tasted sweet and it was still very firm. I thought to myself, everybody likes a happy ending, but we don't belong together.

Afterward

After I finished *American Trash*, I sent it to my college teacher. Here's what she said:

CORNELL UNIVERSITY
ITHACA, N.Y. 14853-3201
607-255-6800
FAX 607-255-6661

DEPARTMENT OF ENGLISH   GOLDWIN SMITH HALL

9 December 2000

Dan Dubelman
█████████████████████████
███████████████████████

Dear Dan—

Thanks very much for your letter and the novel and CD of AMERICAN
TRASH. I'm glad to know that you're continuing to write and make
music; I always admire people who can be productive in different
genres, as some of the best artists have been.

I'm sorry to say, though, that I found your novel somewhat
fragmentary and inconclusive, though full of good moments, and I
don't think I can give you a blurb. Nevertheless I wish you
success in all your enterprises.

With best wishes,

Alison Lurie

The end.

About the Author

After graduating from Cornell, Dan Dubelman received his MA in fiction from Johns Hopkins. He moved to L.A. and worked for The Fox Kids Network. While producing a *Casper* (the friendly ghost) web site for Fox, Dr. Dan met Vickie, who was the liaison for Universal Cartoon Studios. They have been collaborating ever since.

About the Music

Betty used American, acoustic guitars from Elvis, had a party with Dion, and the hotties were dirty dancing to Bernard's fat backs.

Bernard "Pretty" Purdie (Steely Dan, Aretha Franklin, Ray Charles) shook Betty's world when he laid down the drums and co-produced the NYC *American Trash* sessions. The Groovemaster, Jerry Jemmott (BB King, King Curtis, Roberta Flack), turned the world from black and white to color with his animated bass parts. Part of American history, these two musical giants played on many of the Atlantic records that we've all listened to so many times. As Casey Stengel said, "you can look it up."

Jerry Jemmott met Dr. Dan in a recording session when Dan was seventeen. Later, when they needed a drummer for a gig at New York's Bitter End (the one-time home of Bob Dylan), Jerry introduced Dr. Dan and Purdie. Like the Highwaymen they are, they recently started to run together again.

Dr. Dan was fifteen when his father introduced him to **Richie**

Cannata (Elton John, Beach Boys, Billy Joel). Richie would stop by Dan's gigs to jam, playing sax lines and piano riffs that danced over the grooves—just like the ones he laid down here on Betty Dylan's *American Trash* CD.

Vickie was in Venus Con Carne, a band that had just appeared on a hot television show called *Ellen*, when she met Dan. After hearing him play "Okay" with Purdie and Jemmott, Vickie decided to take over his band. She has been the lead singer ever since.

Marvin Etzioni did a combination George-Martin to the head, Phil-Spector jab to the body on Betty. Marvin produced records for the Counting Crows, Toad the Wet Sprocket, and Lone Justice, etc.

A Note from the Producer
"Meet Betty Dylan. This isn't Bob or Jakob. This is Betty Dylan. Betty Dylan is Vickie and Dr. Dan. Bonnie Bramlett meets Lou Reed. A cactus rose in New York City. Country and Eastern. The East Coast girls are hip and I really dig Betty Dylan."

—Marvin Etzioni

Song Lyrics

Track 1

AMERICAN TRASH
WRITTEN BY MARVIN ETZIONI, DAN & VICKIE DUBELMAN

Have you got a TV the size of a flag...American Trash
There's nothing to see so get off your ass...American Trash
Kansas City wine and a pocketful of cash...American Trash
It's Saturday night but it ain't gonna last...American Trash
Not so fast baby, what do you think you're doing...American Trash
Where's your ID, who do you think you're fooling...
American Trash
Baby, we were born in the USA...American Trash
Little Norma Jean threw it all away...American Trash
I'm tall as Texas and real as rain...American Trash
New York's a go-go, love is strange...American Trash
Who's that driving a gold Cadillac...American Trash
Into a Motel 6 where the Bibles are black...American Trash
I'm a gonna tell you how it's gonna be...American Trash
I'm gonna give my love to me...American Trash
And that's that.

Track 2

TOMPKINS SQUARE PARK
WRITTEN BY DAN & VICKIE DUBELMAN

They got baby in a carriage by the dope guy in the park
They got baby in a carriage by the dope guy in the park

Down at Tompkins, down at Tompkins Square Park

They got baby in a carriage by the dog run in the park
They got baby in a carriage by the dog run in the park
Down at Tompkins, down at Tompkins Square Park

When it rains in the park and it starts to get dark
Then it's time to go home grab a bag go alone
A complete unknown and you're not even stoned
What's that shadow in the dark on Avenue B

Don't let those people fool you,
they're not really as scary as they seem
Don't let those people fool you,
they're not really as fucked up as they seem
Down at Tompkins, down at Tompkins Square Park

Track 3

OKAY
WORDS BY DAN & VICKIE DUBELMAN AND ERIC BOTWINIK
MUSIC BY DAN & VICKIE DUBELMAN

Six months of love
One week of hate
Now there's nothing to hold onto
And a long time to wait
Hesitate, incarcerate

Nothing will change cuz I'm on my own
Nothing will change cuz I'm all alone
Everything will be okay
Everything will be alright
Everything will be okay
Everything will be alright

I want to cry
But I don't know how
I'm great at getting hurt
Yeah, I'm great at hiding my pain
You know it's getting late
You know I have to go

Well I'd like to hang around a little while but
Open the door cuz I'm nobody's whore

Track 4

VIOLET TRACKS
WORDS BY DAN & VICKIE DUBELMAN AND JOANNA DEHN
MUSIC BY DAN & VICKIE DUBELMAN

Now I'm feeling nervous, but I'm feeling pretty good.
Now I'm on my own, I never thought I could.
Didn't think I'd make it, but I always knew I should.
Never really certain just where I stood.

You don't know what you've got until it's gone.
You never realized that I could be strong.
Now I'm traveling down a violet track.
And I realize there's no looking back.

She said she loved me, that she'd get me high.
One day the two of us could sail away forever.
No one ever pleased her, she only wanted me.
She said we could be true, and I said I believed her.

Track 5

HARD COUNTRY
WRITTEN BY DAN & VICKIE DUBELMAN

Hard country, got it good
Honky-tonks and Robin Hood
Truck drivers and railroad tracks
My dog just died, and my ex-wife's back
My cowboy Cadillac has got a flat
I'm out of smokes but I got some jack
But most of all, we're not doing smack

Jail break, prison guard
Gonna join a band but it's too hard
Johnny Cash, the man in black
Country licks and chicken shack
Jump down a time hole, fall back to Waco

Buddy Holly's bad lands, Waylon Jennings' jughouse band

Track down Shania Twain
She's a relief pitcher for the Atlanta Braves
Call me when you've got the craze
A country version of "Purple Haze"
Laugh while the laughin's good and pray when you're Robin Hood
Choke down that kit cat smile, reinvent yourself as the holy child

Track 6

ASLEEP & AWAKE
WRITTEN BY DAN & VICKIE DUBELMAN

Caught between asleep and awake
I can't sleep and I won't fake it
Caught between asleep and awake again

It's 3 a.m., lover, you're naked in bed
Awake, asleep, I like to give head
Innocent smile and nonchalant style
C'mon baby, and hang with me for a while

My only solace is to stay in play
I've got the urge to run away
I hope I don't fade away, back into Saturday
Until then, baby, please stay

Mrs. Tiger will be your wife
She'll sleep with you for half of your life
Tiger's stripes and a Sargent's wife
Sargent's stripes and a busy life

Track 7

MR. ROCK AND ROLL
WRITTEN BY DAN & VICKIE DUBELMAN

Mr. Rock and Roll, he's got soul

He's Mr. Rock and Roll, jam all night
He's got a sixty-four black Strat, you got that right

The blues burns his hands on the guitar
He plays with his teeth, he's a rock and roll star

He's Mr. Rock and Roll, he likes Loose Lucy
When they make love, she gets sweet and juicy
The blues that's what he sings
He's Mr. Rock and Roll, so pass him the bing

He's Mr. Rock and Roll, he sold out
Play gigs, sell beer, no doubts
He's turning and twisting like ol' Doctor Dan
He's drowning in a sea of sand

Track 8

LAST NIGHT (WAS THE LAST STRAW)
WRITTEN BY DAN & VICKIE DUBELMAN

Last night was the last straw
Last night was the last straw
Last night was the last straw

Well I won't cry and I won't whimper anymore
I'm gonna lay that nubile busboy/pretty waitress on the floor
So before you come knockin' on my door
I guess I better warn you what's in store

Well I won't cry and I won't whimper anymore
I'm gonna lay that pretty waitress/pretty waitress on the floor
So before you come knockin' on my door
I guess I better warn you what's in store

Last night was the last straw
Now I've got to lay down the law
Don't come around here anymore
This thing has gotten out of hand
If nobody's gonna make a stand
Then I'm the one that's gonna have to take command
I guess I can't take you foolin' around
Lovin' others while I'm on the ground
Listen to my heart, a sorry sound

Track 9

SOMEWHERE IN THIS HEART OF MINE
WRITTEN BY DAN & VICKIE DUBELMAN

She cooed up like Eve from the
Garden of Eden
She leaned in close,
and touched her lips with my neck
She smiled like a tigress, I kissed her hand
I crawled like a viper, she stood like a lamb.
I've got something to play, but it's not me
I won't call it a catastrophe

Somewhere in this heart of mine

I laughed so hard, I couldn't catch my breath
He fell to his knees, tried to touch my dress
Heard him hiccup, he was on a drunk
Heard him playing Thelonius Monk.
If I could find a way out of here
I'd leave in the night, try to hide my fear.

Somewhere in this heart of mine

Her old man wasn't happy about his possession
He felt alone as she was caressing
My hand as we thought about the morning apart
"I'll be with my husband but he doesn't touch my heart."
If love could last then surely this would
But it doesn't last no one guaranteed it could.

Somewhere in this heart of mine

Track 10

YOUR CHEATIN HEART
WRITTEN BY HANK WILLIAMS SR.

Track 11

THE COP
WRITTEN BY DAN & VICKIE DUBELMAN

I am a cop
You are a criminal
I take what I take
You are my prisoner
Your sentence is minimal
And right in the gut
So take it back but pay me in cash

I am a baby blue officer
You're fucking with the law
I am an insatiable lover
I'm fucking with my hat

You are a cherry-topped woman
Integral, integral.
I am a dreaded police car
You're fucking with the law

I'll blow your face off
I'm just holding back
Step out of the car, son
Step out of the car
Don't make me whip you good
Step out of the car, son
Step out of the car

Track 12

DON'T TELL ME WHAT TO DO
WRITTEN BY DAN & VICKIE DUBELMAN, AND ADAM DUBOV

I walked in to find you vacant
And you walked out on the pavement
So I checked out through the bathroom window

Don't tell me what to do

She flew in for the engagement
And you freaked out at the arrangement
So I checked out through the bathroom window

Don't tell me what to do

I walked in to find you vacant
And you walked out on the pavement
She stepped in and she made that statement
So I checked out through the bathroom window

Don't tell me what to do

Track 13

FREE DAY
WRITTEN BY DAN & VICKIE DUBELMAN

It's Independence Day
It's a free day
Make a loud noise
I'm gonna get drunk
It's a free free day

"Happy Independence Day," he says gleefully to the maid
There's not much you need to do to do work
She wants to get by, buy something, not be bought
And he's for sale too
She works for nicer people
Each in his own way
Inadvertently creating
James Joyce or Jessie James like
The outlaw sees more action in Hollywood

Twilight blowing amber light on our porch
With the darkness, I'm working on evasion again
Denial of mortality
You see, I'm not a lazy poet
And, thus, drunken, Invarness or something
Baudelaire might say
Pretty in French
Anyway the point is
Drunk on the night
With its lilac smell of warm night

The sky is falling, I swear
Wild cherries look red in the garden

We didn't worry about baseball or hot dogs
It was Independence Day and he fell flat on his face
Oh, yes, flat on his face
He poured himself a double Stoli and OJ
Some air conditioner water fell on his already sweating brow

Track 14

FAREWELL SHOW
WRITTEN BY DAN & VICKIE DUBELMAN

Hey, mama, can I come home tonight
I need a place to lay in the warm white light
The band is over, they're kicking me out
And Jerry Dog, that drummer
He was laughing, I don't know what about

I got nowhere to stay, mama
The weekend now or maybe one day
I got nowhere to go
Thursday night's the farewell show

Twelve people came
And the Joey Blow Man turned me on
And Crazy Nancy came by
She even tore off her shirt on the last song
Count my money when the crime is through
Cut off my fingers and paste 'em back together with Elmer's Glue

The change finally came
And I switched my path
I took the road more taken
I got tired of breaking my back
And then the man came by
and offered me my assets back
All he wanted was the key to my shack

Acknowledgements

Betty Dylan thanks the following profusely. We love you. We are grateful to the Universe for sending you our way.

The Alley, Amp Rehearsal Studios, Mike Anastasio, Larry Bader, The Bard Family & The Chelsea Hotel, John Barth, Billy Bear, Kahil Kwame Bell, Andy Bottelson, Charlie Bragg, Robert Brink, Richie Cannata, Yu Chiang Cheng, Joan Colee, Complete Music, Michael Covitt, Jeff Cox, Eddie Daniels, Lynn Davis, Frank Distaso, Elaine Dubelman, Rachel, Bobby, Juliana, Deborah & Michael Eddy, Marvin Etzioni, Bob & Dylan at Fahrenheit Studio, Jun Falkenstein, Christopher Farrell, Claudia Field, Russell Fine, Wood Fowler, Bruce & Jerry Foxworth, Mike Galaxy, The Green Dragon, Jim Griffin, Bernie Grundman, Randy Guss, Andrew Harty, Sean Healy, Phyllis Hoefler, Eric Horn (wherever you are), Robin Hurley, Jerry "The Groovemaster" Jemmott, Shane Johnson, Patty Jones, Jesse Kanner, Katie & Patrick Kearney, The Keegan Lloyd family, Dave Kilner, Mark Tapio-Kines, Gaylynn Kiser, Dave Knight, Keith Lambeth, Marshall & Sarah Langer, David Lipsky, Linda Lorence, Alison Lurie, Ronnie Mack, TC Markel, Pamela Massey, Mr. Master, Mike McCalla, Tom McKenzie, Stan Mitchell, Robert Smith and Musician.com, Jennifer Nash, Noah Newman, Alex Olmedo, Kenny Panchuk, Bernard "Pretty" Purdie, Mia Roberts, The Wroman, Joe Romersa, The Roxy, Ann Johns Ruckert, Omar Sebastian, Jeff Sedacca, Lonnie Sill, Paul Slansky, Liz Dubelman & The G, Fortune Smith, Rick Smith, Robert Smith, Nikki Sweet, Caleb Sherman and Unique Recording Studios, Dave Vaught, Tony Viamontes, Dr. Villareal, Kurt Walther, West L.A. Rehearsal Studios, Rich & Caryn Yaker, Ziggy

Credits

Vocals: **Vickie Dubelman & Dr. Dan**
Lead guitar: **Dr. Dan**
Rhythm guitar on tracks 3, 5, 6, 12, 14: **Vickie Dubelman**
Drums: **Bernard "Pretty" Purdie**
Bass: **Jerry "The Groovemaster" Jemmott**
Sax on track 4 and piano on track 7: **Richie Cannata**
Background vocals and claps on track 1: **Jerry Jemmott,
Bernard Purdie, Dr. Dan and Vickie Dubelman**

Executive Producers: **Dr. Dan & Vickie Dubelman**
Producer: **Marvin Etzioni**
Book/CD concept developed by **Marvin Etzioni**
Co-producer NY sessions: **Bernard "Pretty" Purdie**

Engineered and kick-ass old-school tape-editing by
Tony Viamontes
Assistant Engineer: **Mike McCalla**
Mixed by **Tony Viamontes, Dr. Dan & Vickie Dubelman**
Recorded live at **Unique Recording Studios**, New York, NY
Mastered by **Bernie Grundman** at Bernie Grundman Mastering,
Hollywood, CA
Pre-mastering by **Dave Vaught**

Art direction and design by **Fahrenheit Studio**
Cover portraits of Betty Dylan by **Max S. Gerber**
Inside book photography by **Jesse Kanner**

REGIONAL
AMERICA

fahrenheit studio

Web Sites

Betty Dylan
http://www.BettyDylan.com

Daz Unlimited
http://www.DazUnlimited.com

Marvin Etzioni
http://www.RadicalNote.com

Fahrenheit Studio
http://www.Fahrenheit.com

Max Gerber
http://www.msgphoto.com

Bernie Grundman Mastering
http://www.berniegrundmanmastering.com

Jerry Jemmott
http://www.JerryJemmott.com

Jesse Kanner
http://www.epistrophy.com

Musician.com
http://www.Musician.com

Bernard Purdie
http://www.BernardPurdie.com

Regional America
http://www.RegionalAmerica.com

Unique Recording Studios
http://www.uniquerecording.com